# Books by Nicholas Christopher

Poetry

*In the Year of the Comet* (1992)
*Desperate Characters: A Novella in Verse & Other Poems* (1988)
*A Short History of the Island of Butterflies* (1986)
*On Tour with Rita* (1982)

Fiction

*The Soloist* (1986)

Anthology (as Editor)

*Under 35: The New Generation of American Poets* (1989)

# IN THE
# YEAR
# OF THE
# COMET

POEMS BY

# NICHOLAS
# CHRISTOPHER

VIKING

VIKING
Published by the Penguin Group
Viking Penguin, a division of Penguin Books USA Inc.,
375 Hudson Street, New York, New York 10014, U.S.A.
Penguin Books Ltd, 27 Wrights Lane, London W8 5TZ, England
Penguin Books Australia Ltd, Ringwood, Victoria, Australia
Penguin Books Canada Ltd, 10 Alcorn Avenue, Suite 300,
Toronto, Ontario, Canada M4V 3B2
Penguin Books (N.Z.) Ltd, 182–190 Wairau Road,
Auckland 10, New Zealand

Penguin Books Ltd, Registered Offices:
Harmondsworth, Middlesex, England

First published in 1992 by Viking Penguin,
a division of Penguin Books USA Inc.

10 9 8 7 6 5 4 3 2 1

LIBRARY OF CONGRESS CATALOGING IN PUBLICATION DATA
Christopher, Nicholas.
    In the year of the comet : poems/by Nicholas Christopher.
    p.   cm.
    ISBN 0-670-83963-9
    I. Title.
    PS3553.H754I5   1992
    811'.54—dc20   91-16153

Printed in the United States of America
Set in Simoncini Garamond
Designed by Francesca Belanger

*for Constance*

# Contents

## IV. In the Year of the Comet

# I. SUN

# Outside Perpignan in Heavy Rain

The trees sway darkly
along the black wall with its vines.
For shelter, a cat squeezes
between the steel bars over a window.
This is where the caretaker lives,
catty-corner to the cemetery,
with a door the color of stone.

We've just descended the mountains,
windshield wipers slapping mud
while we talked about the acrobat
who was in the papers in Barcelona
yesterday: how he attempted
to perch blindfolded on the highest
steeple of the Gaudí cathedral.

Through the gate, in the first
row of gravestones, a statue
depicts a young woman
raising her hand to her face:
the mortuary sign for a suicide.
Is she about to touch her forehead?
to tear out her hair?
to dig her nails into her cheek?
to stifle a cry
or make the sign of the cross?

In this life which is the only life
it is a gesture we see every day.
You say someone in a position
to know told you it's easy
to learn about these things
without learning anything at all.
Without ever running out of questions.
When that acrobat fell in bright sunlight,
did all the women in the street raise
their hands to shield their eyes?

# Green Chair on a Fire Escape in Autumn

In summer a girl sat
there every afternoon
in a yellow bikini,
fedora, and wraparound
sunglasses, oblivious of
the traffic, skimming
magazines, smoking Cheroots
and sipping Campari
beside her calico cat
who dozed on the windowsill
beneath the cloud-print
curtains while pale clouds
sailed out to sea
and the sun blasted
the bricks so hard dawn
to dusk that a fine red
dust swirled the streets.

Until one day she moved
away, taking the curtains
and the cat but leaving
her chair—still facing
southward to catch
the rays of the sun
which no longer rose high
enough to clear the water
towers of the building
across the street;
and this morning when
a sudden downpour
stopped me under an awning,
and the chair, spattered
with yellow leaves, shone
like fresh enamel against
the dull sky, I wished
she were sitting there
again, startled by the rain

into glancing down
for once, just long enough
to reveal her eyes,
which must be green.

# Epitaph on a Dictator

He was wearing a white tie,
cream-colored suit,
and no blindfold
when they led him
before a firing squad
on Christmas Day
in a rubbled courtyard
full of starving chickens.
All his ministers were forced
to drink strychnine
while handcuffed together
in a meat freezer.
For twenty-four years
he kept a clove of garlic
over his heart, on a chain,
to ward off the Evil Eye,
and he had the National
Orchestra play Wagner
when he swam laps
in the floating natatorium
on his private lake.
His office with its fifty-foot
ceiling and marble pillars
was adorned with six portraits,
twelve busts, and a mural
of himself (heroic on a
battlefield), and his dozens
of uniforms, rainbowed with
medals, hung wrinkle-free
in a refrigerated closet.
In the "out" box on
his desk there were
closeups of naked girls.
(Had the "in" box at some
point contained photos
of the same girls clothed?)
He was a gun collector

and voyeur extraordinaire
(entire brothels monitored
by his secret cameras)
and also a connoisseur of jade,
with predictably expensive
tastes in Scotch, sports
cars, and all things silk.
He boasted he would never
have changed places
with any man anywhere,
even born as he was
in a dirt-floor shack
on the lip of a swamp
with bluebottle flies
dancing around his head.
At the stroke of noon,
under a gunmetal sky,
while the statues of him
in every town and city
were being dynamited,
he died unrepentant
for the thousands
executed in his prisons
and torture chambers,
for the billions of francs
in Swiss banks he had
bled from his citizens,
for the children in work camps
(the lucky ones)
and the others stricken
with polio and AIDS,
died wetting his pants
with three words on his lips:
"Trust no one."

# An Island

Sitting in the shade
of a plane tree
sipping mint tea,
you watch the square empty
in the scalding heat,
dogs lapping at
the mosaic fountain
built for the townspeople
by a penitent Turkish
pirate, and girls
in turbans balancing
baskets of almonds
on their heads,
and the eucalyptus
fronds so still atop
their towering trunks
that they appear to be
painted onto the cloud
which has been frozen
overhead since dawn.
The bank is closed,
and the two cafés,
and the kiosks.
You would be alone
if it were not
for the middle-aged
German doctor at
a nearby table who
is making his two
daughters conjugate
irregular Greek verbs.
You write a postcard,
which later you forget
to mail, and study
a map, checking off
the four churches
(out of forty-seven)

you have not yet visited,
and then light a cigar,
thinking of all
the people you left
behind the first time
you came to this
place, and how few
you left behind now.
Ten years ago you sat
under this tree
and gazed down
the white alley
between the church
and the post office,
past the lime trees
on the promenade,
through the rickety gates
of the seawall onto
that same flashing blue
rectangle of open sea
and felt for an instant
(spiraling away from
yourself like a kite)
that the exquisite current
of light and color
tingling along the thread
of your optic nerve
had distilled and unified
the entire world
in a single image—
and you connected
to it for once.
But if you hoped to
recreate that connection
by reassembling its
elements, you were
bound to be disappointed,
not least of all
because you are only
nominally the same person
you were back then;

and as you glance up,
a boy on a bicycle
with a parrot on his shoulder
speeds across the square,
and one of the German
girls, tugging at her
blond braid, stares after
him wide-eyed, a smile
playing on her lips
as she intones
*I want, you want, he wants*
in the saddest voice
you have ever heard.

# Reading the Sunday Comics,
# Summer 1963

## *1. Gasoline Alley*

Smiling young men with bulging biceps
who change your flat tire
and never dirty their white coveralls.
The girl from the coffee wagon
in her checkered apron
who leans against the soda machine
happily chewing gum.
No one having sex.
Or wanting it.
Lawns and flower beds without weeds
set back on tree-lined streets.
Everything orderly.
Every surface polished.
Every human being as easy
to take apart and reassemble
as a car engine.
A universe of cleanly moving parts
that would have pleased Descartes.
So that, after lunch, at the baseball field,
a boy washing down chocolate bars
with chocolate milk
will rub his rabbit's foot
and pitch a no-hitter
into the ninth inning
of a scoreless game
and then lose it on a bloop single.
Good-naturedly learning a moral lesson.
Then going home to find
a hot supper waiting for him.
On both sides of the railroad tracks
a community of honest men
doing an honest day's work.
No one dying.

Someone always telling a familiar joke
in the end, while the sun sets,
and everybody laughing.


## 2. Blondie

The harried, hysterical housewife
in need of a therapist
in a world where there is no therapy.
Her husband the diligent oaf,
with hair parted down the middle,
who is afraid of his boss.
Her daffy daughter and bumbling son,
who could be youthful twins
of their parents.
She forgets things everywhere:
hats and handbags,
pancakes on the skillet,
irons burning holes in shirts.
She likes bubble baths on hot afternoons.
She shops.
Late at night, when she's taken off
her polka-dot dress
and put on a polka-dot robe,
her husband is making one of his famous
sandwiches, sixteen inches high
(salami, baloney, cheese and onions,
olives, eggs, bacon and pickles),
in the brightly lit kitchen
with the half-moon nestled in the window.
She pours herself a glass of milk
and sits at the table
to watch him eat.
Nothing will ever change for her.
Just once, she would like to sleep
in the nude—with someone else.

## 3. Betty and Veronica

Girls with perfect breasts
driving by a sparkling lake
in a red convertible.
Listening to rock and roll.
Combing their hair.
Eating cheeseburgers and drinking shakes
without ever losing their figures.
One a blonde, the other a brunette.
Carefree and flirtatious.
With beautiful teeth.
They will never witness a crime
or enter a voting booth.
Never go to college
or work in an office
or feel their youth slip away.
Never suffer the griefs
of childbirth, illness or divorce.
For all eternity
boys in letter sweaters
will give them signet rings
and fight for the privilege
of taking them
to drive-ins and proms.
In a life of perpetual sunshine
they never sleep, never tire,
their eyes wide with an astonishment
that never ends.
A kind of passion.


## 4. Dondi

The brooding orphan boy
passed among strangers
who live in gloomy houses.
His suitcase always packed.
His wide mournful eyes.
His blue-black hair with the cowlick.

His life that is a progression
of darkening adjectives.
His dog who is also ineffably sad.
Where will Dondi end up
and how alone will he be,
forever choking back tears
cold as water cupped from deep
in the North Atlantic.
It pained me
that I never liked him.

# Drinking Cold Water
# on the Acropolis at Lindos

The cicadas clatter among star weeds and dust.
No clouds cross the skillet sky.
The temple's marble retains its translucence,
the color of wheat on fire—
like the hair of the girls
who (to beating drums and shrill cries) jumped
from the precipice to the reefs
below, those rows of shark's
teeth laced with foam.
This is Aphrodite's place.
The white birds wheel slowly in the haze,
and the sun is a mirror, tilted to blind.
The bleached sea stretches away south,
to Africa, but filling my cup
from a battered canteen,
raising it to my lips and closing my eyes,
I shiver as light, not water, races
down my throat, into my limbs.
You told me the light was everything here.
Now I see it.

# Notes Toward a History of Imperialism

Our captain Gonzalo Pizarro
ate of the Indians' mushroom
beneath a branchless tree
on the 12th of November 1559
in the jungles of Amazonia
by the River of the Jaguarundi
and glimpsed an army of God's
angels ascending a waterfall
in which fish with transparent wings
fluttered in clouds, like butterflies.

From the west, the rain blows in
sheets, hotter than blood, stinging
like salt, as it lashes our faces
and riddles our boots with worms.
With muskets, sabers, and bare
hands we have committed terrible
crimes in the name of King Philip.
Where villages stood, we left charred
ground: men and women slaughtered;
children enslaved and sold downriver;

the girls raped, out of earshot
of the priests in our party,
who have witnessed all other
atrocities without blinking an eye
(and who insist on Fridays
that we abstain from flesh
and eat the river's eyeless fish).
Drunk by noon, with fevers scalding
our brains and birds clattering,
we slash corridors through the swamps.

We suffer no remorse, but, still,
we are afraid to pray: what
would become of us if we did

open our hearts, even to a god
who (apparently) forsakes the innocent?
Somewhere coals await us that will
make this heat feel like ice.
In his pouch, with its royal seal,
Pizarro has a map of El Dorado,
where the streets, impregnated with sun,

shine gold through the night,
and every window is a mirror,
reflecting only the good in men—
even men like us—and the stairways
in its towers lead directly to clouds
where music, not water, rains down
and makes the gold flowers grow.
In this green maze we come back
on ourselves a hundred times—
our own scorched faces unrecognizable.

At night, if men could fly over
the trees' canopy, our fire—
the hub around which we sleep in
a wheel—must seem like a match
struck at the bottom of the sea.
Only Pizarro lies apart, his pouch
for a pillow, his sword across his chest,
uneasy in his sleep; tonight we can
hear him crying out to his brother
who crucified Atahualpa on a mountaintop.

Perhaps it is the mushroom he took
from the belt of an Indian we hanged
that makes him scream so, filling
his dreams with volleys of arrows
and those man-sized vipers that hang
like vines, waiting to seize us at dawn.
With his commission beneath his head
(to pillage the City of Gold for Spain),
Pizarro knows as we plunge into this
blinding sunlight, like snow rushing

.  .  .  .  .

into a flame, that he will be first
to die when we reach our real destination,
beside boiling waterfalls, and angels
with the faces of children surround us,
their eyes flashing like knives.

# Near Bridgeport,
# Behind a Train Wreck, at Dawn

The abandoned house
on Railroad Avenue—
from these elevated
tracks I can see
right through it,
a set of dirty blue
windows on each side,
and in between,
in pale light,
the ghosts stretched out
on metal beds,
their feet, clear
as ice, protruding
from taut sheets.
The bureau lies under
a snowfall of dust;
its broken mirror,
tilted sharply,
reflects the remains
of a bathroom
across the hall.
Spider webs hang
like tapestries
from the ceiling,
and below a swallows'
nest (long abandoned
itself) in one corner,
petrified droppings,
dense as hieroglyphics,
cover the wallpaper.

Behind the house,
swaying through the windows,
a jungle of gingko
and locust trees,
vines snaking up their

trunks, glows red,
then orange, as the sun
rises above the stacks,
towers, and storage
tanks of the factories
looming in the distance,
silver-green, almost watery,
beneath gunpowder clouds.
An hour ago, a half
mile back, as we
crossed an iron bridge
over the filthy river,
I glimpsed those same
factories from another angle,
through the rusted
trelliswork and cables,
and deep in their midst
(invisible to me now)
a gray steeple
with a gold cross
jutted into the sky.
There was not a single
house, store, or office
building in sight—
just the factories
and the church,
its pews (perhaps)
filled with workers
with grim shining faces
and calloused hands
who put in sixteen-hour
shifts and then do
nothing but pray.

Four hours ago, in Boston,
I missed the train
before this one
by less than a minute
because my taxi,
swerving to avoid
a stray dog

in a dark intersection,
ran a red light
and was stopped
by the police.
So instead of being
a passenger—or casualty—
in the derailment
(our conductor informs
us that two people
were killed and dozens
injured when a mass
of hissing wires
entangled the cars),
I'm clutching
a container of coffee
and a stale doughnut
and watching the sunlight,
yellow now, flood through
that room toward me,
gilding the furniture
and emptying the mirror
and pouring currents
of light through the ghosts—
electrifying them for an instant—
as a lone swallow,
hovering by the window,
streaks into the trees.

# Xaniá, 1983

*1.*

So pure the rain
on the black streets,
a sudden downpour at 4 A.M.
and no one to see it.

*2.*

Thirteen wildflowers in a
pitcher by the window,
one of them dripping—orange—
on a broken stem.

*3.*

In the steaming courtyard
a bee circles the head
of the marble horse
while bells peal across the city.

*4.*

From the harbor, the blue
machinery of the sea:
constantly in motion
without moving parts.

*5.*

Sunlight showers the hillside
cemetery, pooling and running
like a river of gold,
down into the dark vineyard.

6.

At the rear of the funeral
procession an infant swaddled
in blankets, in the arms of
a small girl, cries out suddenly.

# Diptych

*A Sea Gull*
far from sea
circled over me
as I lay in
the August sun,
rose along
a steep spiral
silhouetted against
a grape-colored
cloud until he was
just a pinpoint
of black.
And the sun ferocious,
its rays streaming
out from behind
the cloud at
another angle,
like the beneficent
rafters of light
supporting Heaven
in Raphael's paintings.
And the curved sky
intensely blue.
And the wind rushing.
Later, after I
closed my eyes,
that cloud must
have blown eastward
slowly until it
reached the sea,
sailing high over
the iron waves.
As for the gull,
I was sure it

was not a gull
at all but
the soul of
someone who
had died that
afternoon somewhere
in the enormous
landlocked city
and then ascended.
So quickly.


2.

*A V-Shaped Formation of Crows*
slides in from sea
across the city sky,
great wings flapping
in unison
in the violet dusk
as they pass high
over the glittering
suspension bridge
where this morning,
while the bells
of the buoys clanged
200 feet below,
a girl opened
her umbrella,
kicked off her shoes,
and with a flower
in her teeth walked
along the railing
never looking down
until she reached
the far side
and slipped, tumbling
backward, landing
hard on the cement
walkway, her face
dark with disappointment

as the flower flew off
in the other
direction on a gust
of wind and alighted
on the freezing
choppy waters
of the river
and was carried out
to sea on a succession
of crow-black waves—
inverted V's tipped
white, flashing
in the red sun.

# II. MOON

# In the Country

The lamplight, whirring
with mosquitoes, streams
out the screen door,
across the lawn,
and enters the forest.
Mist is rising from the ferns.
All the windows are open
and the wind is blowing
through the house,
over the meadow,
and rippling the surface
of the lake.
When your voice breaks
the stillness,
my pulse jumps—
as if I'm leaning
over the roof
of a tall building,
the full moon blazing
in my eyes.
One stormy night in Rome
I sat up for hours
with a girl I met
on the Paris express.
She, too, spoke with
that shivering cadence
in the blue darkness—
about her family in Spain,
her father the blind poet
and his whitewashed
house on a cliff
overlooking the sea.
In the morning
I opened my eyes
and she was crouched
at the foot of the bed
reciting his poems

from memory.
Years later, I heard
her father had been imprisoned
and her husband and son
had died of cholera;
committed to a sanitarium,
her hands and feet swollen
and her hair
falling out in sheaves—
dry as wheat—
she crept up to the roof
one night during a blizzard,
waited for the bells
to ring Vespers,
and jumped.

You've brought all this
back to me.
The thunder and lightning,
and the cats crying
like frightened angels
on the Via Cavour
while rain drilled the rooftops.
I tell myself it happened
a long time ago
and that here (miles
from the nearest road)
nothing can touch us,
even as moonlight crosses
the lake and the meadow
and enters the bedroom
window, enfolding you
like a sheet
and carrying you away.

# Vertigo from an Open Window
# Overlooking a Sodium Light

*1.*

In a book published in Buenos Aires
at the turn of the century, I read
that Columbus was convinced the New World
was the site of the Garden of Eden.
He had dreams in which he picked
oranges off overloaded trees,
bit into them, and tasted the milk
of paradise—sweet and bright.
And other dreams in which Oriental
girls in silk pantaloons, with small,
rounded breasts, dug for gold
in deep mines under his direction.
By day, gout-ridden, besotted with rum,
he stamped the quarterdeck,
railing at his men and cursing the sun.
On the ceiling of his cabin
his brother Bartholomew had painted
as enormous octopus, perched on
a mountaintop, a gleaming, upright
sword in each of its tentacles;
over the swords, eight angels hovered.
I lost this book on an airplane
and could never find another copy.

*2.*

Last night on the subway a man
in a bowling jacket, his cheeks
pockmarked, was reading a book
entitled *Sex and the Outer Planets,*
using an orange gum wrapper as a page-marker.
The gum he was chewing vigorously.
On the back of his head, reflected

in the window, the shadow
of a spider crawled rapidly—
like a tattoo come to life.
A puddle was forming around his scuffed
boots, the rainwater dripping from
his cuffs in an irregular syncopation,
each drop setting off a ripple
that caught the violent yellow lights
flashing through the windows
as we screeched along the Lexington
Avenue tunnel deep within
the bedrock of Manhattan Island.
When he got off at Twenty-third Street,
he left his book on the seat;
at Fourteenth Street another man
sat down, opened it to the page marked
by the gum wrapper, and started reading,
tapping his foot in the puddle.


3.

Up and down the narrow street
the trees are black and blue.
Mist drifts in from the river.
The streetlight hisses softly, with a pink glow.
A remote, tingling current runs from my groin
to the base of my skull.
In the tight cave of my thorax
my organs—kidneys, liver, spleen,
and lungs—seem to be pressing
up hard against one another.
No room down there tonight for "feelings,"
for "the soul" in any of its subtle forms.
Is this the first manifestation of serious illness?
A quick foreshadowing of you-know-what?
More to the point, I'm growing dizzy.
Ashes under my tongue.
Wrists pulsing.
In my hand there is a black book
I have never seen before,

which I found on the windowsill
beside my bed.
It is opened to an unnumbered
page containing a single
sentence, vertically:
*You*
*are*
*falling*

# Cancer Ward

The dark plant at the end
of the long corridor
has not been watered for days.
Light streaming through
the venetian blinds encircles
it with bands of dust.
A fly with one wing
hangs from the edge
of the topmost leaf.
Another fly is buzzing a zigzag
up and down the window,
ticking against the glass,
trying to get out.
Beyond a set of double doors,
around a corner,
a man is coughing violently.
Behind another door,
marked NO ADMITTANCE,
a machine is whirring
and a woman is crying.
A car horn sounds faintly
on the street below,
as if it is coming from
many miles at sea,
muffled by dense fog.
Like a ship returning
from those distant islands
where the dead lie shoulder to shoulder
in white sand
under a full moon.
The islands where thousands
of these plants grow
in endless, silent fields
and nothing—not even the black wind—
can ruffle their heavy leaves.

# How Beautiful Was Miranda?

That last night she sat brooding
on the steps of the icehouse.

Blue light streamed out
the small circular window.

On the lake, an empty canoe
was gliding toward the opposite shore.

There was the crack of a rifle through the trees,
and then its echo across the water.

For a moment the insect buzz went dead,
as if someone had thrown a switch.

"That's him," she said, toeing the dirt
with her boot, "shooting at the bottle
he started in on after dinner.
When they're empty, he sets them up
at fifty yards, and he never misses."

Then she moved closer to me,
raising her face up into the circle of light.

And even when I heard him approaching,
calling her name, I didn't let go of her.

# Nine Cities

Glass chimes fashioned in Venice
are tinkling in a window
on the other side of the world
and you can hear them

in Lhasa, where the sapphire
light tints the mountain
peaks at dusk, making
you wince with pleasure

on a New York rooftop
stargazing past the silhouettes
of the water towers
on a night so black you tremble

in Rome under a street lamp
by the Temple of Mars
where the iron eagles glare
and the sparrows sing so sweetly

that you weep in Kyoto on a stone
bench beside rain-drenched ferns,
listening to Mozart's *Requiem*
and sifting through your memories

of Stockholm in winter: skating
across the frozen lake at dawn
and drinking Kir in the park
when the equestrian statues leaped high

suddenly like the dancers in Guayaquil
who work the snow-white beaches
with marimba bands on fiery afternoons,
their hair burning scarlet

as the cactus flowers in Santa Fe
the girls are picking

on the edge of the desert
where all the car radios are blaring

"Moscow Nights" and you're tapping
your foot in time on the other
side of the world—chimes flashing
moonlight in the window.

# Jazz

When my mother was pregnant with me
she worked at a record company
that produced jazz
(jive jump swing & bebop)
and spent many afternoons
that summer and fall
at recording sessions
on the West Side of Manhattan
talking with the musicians between takes
sipping Coca-Cola
eating sandwiches with the engineers
closing her eyes
and tapping her feet to the music
and me there inside her
drums bass piano trumpet & trombone
and all those saxophones
working on my sensibilities
such as they were
like someone at the bottom of a swimming pool
who hears a band playing up above
under the moon on a warm night
taking it in
under the bigger bass of her heartbeat
all those rhythms
and crosscurrents of sound
(and moving to it?)
all those rhythms
I must have been listening for
months later when I was born
my ear cocked for them
in the loud world
and where were they?
all those rhythms

# Rooftop

Across the street tonight
the snow is glazed fast
on the warehouse roof.

As if at any moment
a phalanx of skaters
might dart from the shadows

of the water tower executing
perfect leaps, pirouettes
and figure eights, etching

the ice with their intricate
designs until patterns emerge,
like maps (hopelessly over-
lapping) of their inner lives.

But, instead, dozens of pigeons,
their wings flecked
with moonlight, explode
from the clotted darkness

of the water tower, wheeling
into momentary formations
against the frozen sky,

where those of us quick enough
will read our futures:
the time and place of our deaths,

and even the dreams we'll dream
tonight, sharp gusts hissing
like blades across the window.

# Americana

All the houses are red or green,
with bright yellow roofs.
Birds sing full-throated
in the fruit-laden trees.
Shiny cars line the streets.

But when the sea of night
rolls in from the east
to cover the continent,
over the foothills and factories
and the deep rivers

overflowing with rain,
the men and women
sitting in hot rooms
with tightly drawn drapes
turn off their televisions

and pull down the sheets
and lie side by side in silence
wondering who will save them
from death, and why, and what
it is they're waiting for

if not that, even as an ark,
white as moonlight,
crosses the horizon carrying
the people who escaped a flood
in some distant town.

# Ariadne auf Naxos

The windows are curtained.
Tanks of saltwater line the walls
and in their bright blue light
fish dart among the anemones.
Down a hallway a dog is barking,
and upstairs a woman paces
on a polished floor, clicking
out a message of distress.
A man enters the room, sliding
from shadow to shadow, assuming
the shape of successive objects—
chair, bureau, potted palm . . .
finally merging with the statue
of Bacchus beside a dark screen.
He waits, knowing she will come
to him, despite herself—
her fear of being abandoned again.
At dawn, when the curtains are drawn,
there are no fish in the tanks
and no people in the room;
just a single statue of a woman
with sea-twined hair and a cold smile,
a cluster of grapes in her hand.

# Through the Window of the All-Night Restaurant

across from the gas station
a bus stopped every ten minutes
under the blue streetlight
and discharged a single passenger.
Never more than one.
A one-armed man with a cane.
A girl in red leather.
A security guard carrying his lunch box.
They stepped into the light,
looked left, then right, and disappeared.
Otherwise, the street was empty,
the wind off the river gusting paper and leaves.
Then the pay phone near the bus stop
started ringing; for five minutes it rang,
until another bus pulled in
and a couple stepped off,
their hats pulled down low.
The man walked up the street,
but the woman hesitated,
then answered the phone and stood
frozen with the receiver to her ear.
The man came back for her,
but she waved him away
and at the same moment her hat blew off
and skidded down the street.
The man followed it, holding his own hat,
and the woman began talking into the phone.
And she kept talking,
the wind tossing her hair wildly,
and the man never returned
and no more buses came after that.

# III. CONSTELLATIONS

# Mrs. Luna

Think of an address you've known
for many years, embedded
in your memory—mantra-like—
belonging to a distant
aunt or uncle
whom you've never visited
but to whom you send
a card at Christmas
and from whom you receive
neatly wrapped packages
on your birthday;
or the address of a former
lover or long-lost
friend residing on
an exotically named street
(Royal Alhambra Boulevard)
in an unlikely town
(Nocturne, South Dakota).
It is just such an address
(for you, the abstraction
of a place)
that one day you find
yourself standing before:
a stucco bungalow
on a cul-de-sac
lined with fake cacti
in Las Vegas,
or a gritty row house
with yellow evergreens
in Baltimore,
or a high-rise condominium
with a heart-shaped
swimming pool
in Albuquerque.
And when you discover
it's not at all
what you imagined,

the entire tableau begins
to vibrate, the very
molecules altering themselves
at high speed until
a new image appears,
conforming to your preconceptions,
which (it happens)
have also undergone
a subtle transformation,
and so in the end it's
only you who will change.

And this is something like
what I experienced
the first time I saw
a dead body lying in state,
my childhood neighbor Mrs. Luna,
whom I used to glimpse
daily in her flouncy robe
getting the mail
or paying the milkman
or watering her tiny lawn.
She was a recluse,
partial to Dixieland jazz,
with a smoky whiskey voice
and murky history:
twice widowed, a daughter
in a sanitarium,
a red De Soto convertible
parked by her house
on Sunday nights,
and a barking dog
that no one ever saw—
Mrs. Luna, whom I'd known
for years yet never
known at all,
there before me at age ten
and nothing like what I expected.

# On the Peninsula

Lit from below, the blue water
flows to us on three sides.
Yellow crabs scuttle across the sand
and the moon sails over the mountains.
The stars are set close and bright—
it would take us a dozen human lifetimes,
traveling at the speed of light,
to reach the nearest one.
To reach the seafloor
takes less than a minute;
lungs straining, we glimpse
a million stars pinpointed
in the eyes of the fish,
schools of them hovering
in the beams of our torches
as the currents carry us from shore,
away from the rustling grass
and the deep orchard
and the house where our bodies,
locked fast, turn under a blue sheet.

# Approaching Antarctica

The slate sky is streaked
baby blue
and the sea,
smooth as a mirror,
reflects passing clouds.
The ship's titanium hull
hisses through the ice,
past islands of glass,
her atomic engines
humming to the tune
of a billion atoms
splitting, spitting
forth electrons.
In the prow, a blind
man is clutching
a handful of cherries
while the terns,
crying harshly,
wheel overhead;
in the stern, three
men with binoculars
gaze at the horizon,
the zigzag lightning bolts
and the squalls
wobbling like tops.
The satellite dish
a hundred feet up
is revolving slowly,
heaped with snow,
but still the messages
from the ionosphere,
from satellites
orbiting the Earth
at dizzying speed,
are crackling in,
informing us
of the dangers

we'll encounter tonight—
the icebergs, gale winds,
and treacherous currents—
when the ship, its
portholes glinting topaz,
parts the curtain
of a raging blizzard
and cuts through
miles of ice floes,
the snowflakes flashing
phosphorescent as
fallout, or fireflies,
or volcanic embers
blown south
from the equator,
which no longer seems
so far away;
as if the southern
hemisphere, bowl-shaped
(like one of those
paper models
used to illustrate
a theorem of geometry),
has been folded
over upon itself,
so that the equator
touches a single point:
the South Pole.

Ultimately, at either pole,
or in other places
of vast solitude—
like a small room
in the predawn—
you must keep
in mind Lucretius's
aside (while discussing
the movements of atoms)
that "all life is a
struggle in the dark."
And all men in their dreams

are wrestling their
opposite numbers—
clothed in the colors
of death—
struggling to survive,
to triumph,
and finally to vault
the four walls
of their perceptions
until they free-float
into the heady ether
of that famous sphere
which is everywhere
with a center
that is nowhere.

# Ghosts

At 3 A.M. two girls with scarves
tied around their feet are begging
outside a Chinese restaurant,
jangling coins in paper cups
under the coils of pink neon
that flicker SZECHUAN CUISINE
in the fogged-up window.
Snow is falling fast.
The traffic light at the corner
is rocking in the wind, flashing amber,
but there are no cars in sight.
The sidewalks are empty.
The restaurant has been closed for hours.
Still, the girls are stamping their feet,
stepping this way and that,
as if they were working
within a stream of pedestrians.
And none of them stopping.

# The Pocket Watch

This is the grave of a man
who every day of his life
wore a starched white shirt;
who taught me how
to play solitaire,
and then double solitaire,
in a white room
where the radiator knocked
and a jade plant
grew in a flowerpot
full of bleached stones;
who drank his rye neat
and lit his ten-cent cigars
with the wooden matches
he kept in the saddlebags
of a ceramic elephant;
who carried a small penknife
with a mother-of-pearl
handle on his key chain
to clip those cigars;
who worked at an oyster bar,
shucking shellfish over
a barrel in a rubber apron;
who shaved at 6 A.M. sharp
and salted his food heavily
and didn't eat meat on Friday
yet seldom went to church;
who brought walnuts to
the squirrels in Fort Tryon Park
and preferred Westerns
when he attended matinees
at the RKO Coliseum;
who stuck a carnation
in his lapel on Sundays
and only danced at weddings—
and was a good dancer;
who was married to the same

woman for fifty years
and had three children
and five grandchildren,
only two of whom he lived to see;
who died suddenly thirty
years ago after consulting
his gold pocket watch
engraved with celestial bodies;
the watch his father
sent him from Europe
when he arrived in America
at age thirteen
on an Egyptian freighter
with forty dollars
and a cardboard suitcase;
the watch he was buried with,
which even now, my heels
planted in the stubborn grass
on this windswept hillside,
I can hear ticking
down among his bones.

# Scarlet Lake

Derain, after his wife's
suicide, awoke in the Alps
in a small hotel.
The grass was crazy with bees—
and how the fish
were jumping on the lake!
He gazed over it for hours,
smoking his blunt meerschaum
with the amber stem.
A spider plant hung its
satellites around his head.
Embers hissed in the stove.
In the eggshell demitasse
the coffee grounds swirled
like ocean sediment,
glinting with lights.
He watched the fat cook
amble up through the pines
clutching a pair
of ducks the porter
had ambushed at dawn.
Their bright green feathers
were streaked with mud.
Blood speckled their bills.
When a storm swept in from
the west—from France—
the rain slanting down
hard across the mountains,
only the surface of the lake
remained undisturbed,
placid; very slowly
it turned a deep red.

# South of the Border

He woke up in a car
in Símon Bolívar Plaza
at the stroke of noon
just as three men wearing
cassocks and ski masks
lobbed Molotov cocktails
into the munitions plant
across the capital.

> *He had been dreaming*
> *of a lake in the north*
> *where the wind was sawing*
> *through blocks of ice.*

So he did not hear the explosion
that rang church bells
for miles, and shook
the wings of passing planes,
and shattered suburban windows.

> *When he last visited*
> *that lake, he had not*
> *slept for days.*
> *It was a misty summer*
> *night and he sat on*
> *a platter-shaped boulder*
> *listening to a waterfall*
> *that shone through*
> *the blue trees.*

The men, in work clothes,
were arrested quickly,
two careening along
a mountain road in a van
full of chickens,
the other playing
a harmonica up and down

the immaculate street
in front of police headquarters.

> *But in his dream the night*
> *was clear, and the surface*
> *of the lake was sprinkled*
> *with the mica of starlight.*
> *The pines were snow-laden*
> *and the waterfall was frozen,*
> *rising into the darkness*
> *like a Doric column.*
> *Planting dynamite at its base,*
> *he lit a long fuse*
> *and ran for his life,*
> *and when the ice burst*
> *like a thunderclap,*
> *and the forest flooded,*
> *he woke up behind the wheel*
> *of that car in hot sunlight.*

The police, wearing ski masks,
forced the men to sign
confessions in their own blood.
Then they drove them
to the sea, their wrists
bound with catgut,
made them kneel in the sand,
and pressing rifles to
their temples blew them
into oblivion under a cloud
of screaming gulls.

> *Later, in an empty hotel,*
> *he dozed off listening*
> *to staccato bulletins*
> *on the radio:*
> *the police were searching*
> *for another saboteur,*
> *last seen in a stolen car*
> *in Símon Bolívar Plaza.*
> *When he was awakened*

*at midnight by a sharp*
*knock at the door,*
*the cassocks the dead men*
*had worn were discovered*
*in a first-class compartment*
*on a train that had just*
*crossed the border,*
*into the north.*

# Confessio Amantis

*In the interior of Sumatra the rice is sown by*
*women who, in sowing, let their hair hang loose*
*down their backs, in order that the rice may grow*
*luxuriantly and have long stalks.*
         — J A M E S   F R A Z E R , *The Golden Bough*


Where are those girls now who twenty
years ago, when you were barely twenty,
opened their arms to you on snowy nights
and put the fever into your veins?

One—later a doctor of medicine—
loved to tryst in the kitchen,
on a butcher-block table,
while her mother (a judge)
read the evening paper in the next room.

You can still see clearly the odd
details of her face: a green cloud
hovering in the left iris, a question-mark
scar by the ear, and violet lips

mouthing the songs on the radio
and then whispering your name faster
and faster under the Tiffany lamp
while the dog watched from the corner.

Later, you recounted to her how,
during his conversion, his back to the light,
St. Augustine claimed his eyes,
by which he saw all things illuminated,
were themselves in darkness.

Your shirt around her shoulders,
her knees drawn up into her chest,

she gazed out at the icy trees
in the park and pretended to listen.

In those days you were full of big ideas.
And while snow spun wildly into Manhattan,
your partners already understood
what you only now begin to grasp,

what the girls on more fertile islands
are taught from birth: the only knowledge
that matters, bridging chasms over the long
years, must find its way into ritual
and stop short of words, always.

# Mona Kay

When he sailed away,
he took an overnight bag
and a photograph
of a woman in the desert.

At twilight he circled
the deck and saw nothing
but whitecaps for miles—
a sea of broken glass

splashed with enamel—
and heard nothing but the wind
sweeping the horizon of sound.

Occasionally he glimpsed
a schooner with masts of snow
slide from the mist
and melt away before his eyes.

His ship, the *Mona Kay,*
flew the Moroccan flag
and carried a cargo of iron ore.
He was the lone passenger,

a man in a black coat
who paced his cabin all night—
dining alone, smoking,

and drinking black tea.
Until one day a familiar
face appeared on the deck
of that schooner—a woman

beckoning him from the stern—
and he threw off his coat
and dove into the waves.
They entered his cabin

. . . . .

and found her photograph
tacked over the iced porthole:
his wife who had burned up

with a fever in the Sahara
and was buried in the snow-white sand;
inscribed with a shaky hand, it read:
*Yours forever, Mona Kay*

# April in New York

Vapor is curling from the manhole
like a snake from a basket.
Rain curtains the windows.
A girl made up as Mussolini—
twenty medals across her chest—
waves an Ethiopian flag and goose-steps
to martial music on a flatbed truck.
Behind the wheel, a man in whiteface
wearing a fez whispers sweet nothings
to a blow-up doll of Brigitte Bardot
in a see-through raincoat.
The charcoal sky, smeared purple,
is crisscrossed with sailboats.
It's springtime: from Inwood
to the Battery, the crowds
are restless, tossing confetti.

*2.*

How many false prophets will shamble
from furnished rooms today
to preach the Gospel on littered corners
or thump their Korans in caged windows?
Last night the planet Mars,
ascendant in the west, burnt
a pinhole—ruby-brilliant—
through a curtain of storm clouds.
A girl in a see-through raincoat
was murdered on East Fourth Street
by a panhandler with a mandolin.
His hair was dyed chlorophyll green
and his purple cape was embroidered
with sailboats in a moonlit expanse.
Speaking garbled Ethiopic, he confessed

to the police, but insisted
(through an interpreter)
that it was a crime of passion.


3.

It's the month of suicides.
Everybody wants something
and nobody knows where to get it.
Or why it would make any difference
in the long run if they did.
A man in a green fez and purple zoot suit
has tacked up a photo of Brigitte Bardot
in his cell in the Tombs;
he claims he's a political prisoner
writing the true history of Mussolini's
invasion of Ethiopia in 1936.
Outside his barred window the streets
of Chinatown teem with angry crowds.
A girl in whiteface is strumming
a mandolin in the driving rain
and singing love songs in Italian—
as if her life depended on it.

# Stars

The three *cantiche* of the *Divina Commedia*
close with the word *stelle*
because Dante wanted to emphasize
that the soul, in its long journey,
should aspire always to the highest state of nature.

Empedocles postulated that the energy
churning within stars also powered
the circuits of the human brain,
and that all animate matter on Earth,
at the moment of death, streamed a column
of luminous molecules upward into the heavens.

Poseidonius defined man as "the beholder
and expounder of heaven," his eyes, capable
of examining the remotest constellations,
marvels of nature, "tiny mirrors"
in which immensity is reflected inward.

From a muddy field in Buxton, North Carolina,
these same stars swirl into crescents—
vast wheels drawing us out of ourselves, it's true;
but tonight would we want to leave behind
this cold sea wind, these birds, this thumping
in our chests that echoes like a drumbeat
down to the soles of our feet, grounding us.

# IV. IN THE YEAR OF THE COMET

# The Black Bells from Gina's Farm

The perfume of the white flowers
in the black vase
is giving us vertigo.
All night we've been sitting
at a wooden table in the stone house
waiting for the rain to stop.

Over the mountains the sky has broken
and tridents of lightning
are streaking through the clouds,
rattling off the rocky peaks.

In the next room, three people
are arguing in a language
we don't understand.

Only a word here and there.
And Gina's name, many times.
Goats are kicking in the yard,
dogs are barking, and off where

the darkness deepens, beyond
an orchard crazy with nightingales,
and wheat fields sizzling with insects,

two horses are rearing in a pool
of moonlight. Drowning.
Only after the rain stops,
and the argument, and the restlessness

of the animals, do we feel the iron
weight of silence pressing down
on this island from the sky;

only then do we hear the last pealing
of the black bells from the church

across the mountains, by the sea.
All this time they were ringing,

but only the animals heard them.
Gina died in the village tonight.
If we had heard those bells,

there would have been no quarrel
and you and I would have set out
along the mountain road
hours ago, despite the rain,
clutching those flowers.
Everything might have been different.

# The Stadium at Delphi

This is where Alexander raced against the other kings.
A silver ellipse cut high into the mountain.
Eagles nesting in the cliffs.
A sea of fiery flowers.
At night, sharp echoes trail the wind.
The priests called it the Eye of the Universe,
where all of us—like the blind—can see everything
and be reminded that we know nothing.

# Atlantic Avenue

We ran every red light on the boulevard
and skidded to a stop at the breakwater,
below the old lighthouse.
The waves tumbled in low and black.
Gulls were skimming the foam.
Beyond the jetty, and the buoys,
a white ship slid out to sea.
Passengers lined the decks,
taking a last look at the island.
You reached over and flashed the headlights twice.
Then, as the pilot boat lurched back to harbor,
you leaned away into the shadows.
"We should be on that ship," you said,
"now, before it's too late."

But it was already too late.
That summer no ships were sailing where we had to go.
One night we left the island separately, but not alone.
From the deck, I heard gulls screaming
in the mist, and I glimpsed
the lighthouse, high on its bluff,
flickering like a match in an empty room.

# The Morning of the Funeral

Rain is moving down from the mountains.
In a small trailer by a sand pit,
behind blue venetian blinds,
a girl in a bathrobe is drinking coffee.
Her eyes are fixed on a bowl of oranges.

Her hair is brushed back over her
shoulders and she is talking to herself.
A fly is walking circles around
a drop of honey on the black
(flecked with gold) formica table.

Rays of light glance off the high rises,
their girders creaking like bones.
There are no pedestrians at this hour.
The street cleaners in their white truck,
spraying the gutters, smoke big cigars.

Behind the girl, a black dress revolves
stiffly on a hanger by the Murphy bed.
She has circus posters on the walls:
tigers cleaving hoops of fire; clowns
juggling; trapeze artists; a white horse.

Rossini's *Tancredi*—a scratchy 78-rpm
recording—is playing on her phonograph.
An empty wine bottle is lying in the sink.
When she lights a cigarette, her irises
contract sharply, flecked with gold.

Suddenly rain is hammering the roof
of the trailer, and a boy in white appears,
rolls to the bottom of the sand pit
and lies there with crossed arms,
breathing fast, pretending to be dead.

# Alley Cat Near the Harbor

Once a ship's cat, fed galley scraps,
with a nook among the sailors' bunks,
now he sleeps alone, hollow-ribbed,
beneath broken steps on a sack of rags.
Snow slants through the streetlight,
drifting on the iced pavement,
and the wind whistles along the rattling fence.
But no sound stirs him.
Not the rat, scurrying along a drainpipe.
Not drunks, vagrants, or policemen.
Not even the shopkeeper who leaves him
the poisoned fish he doesn't touch.
Through the long night his ears never
twitch as on the sea-green of his eyelids
he watches ships slide by in open waters,
slowly, under slow white clouds.

# Three Dreams on a Train Riding North

*1.*

I am walking down
an empty New York street
at nightfall, the wind
hissing like static.
In a darkened building
a single light burns
in a high window.
A woman is silhouetted
holding a pair of scissors.
The light goes out
and people in black coats
pour from doorways
and flood the streets.
Rain clouds mask their faces.
Suddenly it is raining
and I have no coat.
An invisible hand grips
my arm and leads me
past a woman on horseback
in bronze brandishing
a two-edged sword.
Overhead, the stars line
the sky in neat strips,
as if they have been cut
out of a sheet of black
paper to which someone
has just set a match;
slowly it burns inward,
toward the full moon.

*2.*

In a parking lot
beside an amusement park

a faceless couple
with hats pulled low
step from a sedan
with blank license plates.
Conversing in a foreign
language, the woman says
my name in passing.
They get into another car
and drive away with all
the windows rolled down
despite the freezing cold.
I board a train and ride
to the end of the line,
and sitting on a bench
in a hot waiting room,
I glimpse an onyx earring
with silver spangles
beside my foot.
I buy a pack of cigarettes,
though I gave up
smoking years ago.
A young woman offers
me a light as a car
screeches up in the blue
mist, its windows thick
with snow and ice.
I step outside and a gust
of wind blows a pillbox
hat into my hands.
Inside the hat is
a photograph of a woman
wearing onyx earrings.
She resembles the woman
in the waiting room,
but she's much older,
with pure white hair.
The car speeds off
and I hear the music
of a carousel, drunken,
beyond the bare trees.

*3.*

In a scorching desert
I am sitting at a marble
table wearing a watch
on each wrist.
The horizon shimmers,
but there is no sun
in the sky.
A phonograph is playing
harsh Egyptian music.
A woman in a red cape
and gloves brings me
a glass of water
and a pair of binoculars
and points to an oasis
where a man dressed
like an admiral,
bound to a stake,
faces a firing squad.
I hear a crack of rifles
and the woman hands me
an admiral's hat
dripping braid and filled
with blood in which
ice cubes are floating,
each of them
reflecting the sun,
risen directly overhead,
out of nowhere.

# Melodrama

*Jupiter descends in thunder and lightning,*
*sitting upon an eagle: he throws a thunderbolt.*
*The Ghosts fall on their knees.*


This is a stage direction from *Cymbeline*.
You'd think all hell was about to break loose—
but it was just a bad dream.
Some toys gone crazy on a riverbank.
Imagine a gout-knobbed nuncle on a painted bird
(wires, papier-mâché & glue) raising
a sputtering lighter to an exploding cigar
while boys in sheets genuflect, smirking.

What we know now, in decline, we knew always
in our bones, with the surety of stones,
of bones embedded for all time in stone:
the music that disturbed the first man's
sleep retains its hard cadence, rains
hot embers off the drums in the sky.

We've come and gone too many times.
Joints swollen, eyes washed-out, and still
in our hearts we're only just beginning,
assuming we have all the time we need, and more.
There is something evil here that runs us ragged. . . .
It's one thing to spar with the stage manager,
quite another to venture naked into the pit,
without clever riposte, no helpful clowns, a full house.

Let our sense of history sustain us then—
the comic-strip pageantry, the textbook captions,
the tattered flags—even as the cornets
sound in Act V, and the extras troop off,
and the river tosses up the head of the murdered fop,
drawing a good laugh every time,
·   ·   ·   ·   ·

the head still blinking glass eyes,
pontificating in its doll's voice,
while the soothsayer declares the Kingdom
to be saved (prince triumphant, princess
betrothed) and Nature reaffirmed . . .
at every river's mouth the head of a fool.

# Easter Morning, Hydra

*1.*

High in the cliffs
on a balcony
overhanging the sea
an old woman unfurls
a red blanket
as the wind blows out
her white hair
like spray.

*2.*

At the harbor
children in white
parade the battlements
of the Crusaders' fortress
and release a bouquet
of balloons
that the wind carries
off into the clouds—
all except a single
red one
which spins down
into the waves
and sparkles
like a drop of blood.

# Magnets

*. . . the body of man is Magneticall, and being
placed in a boat, the vessell will never rest until the
head respecteth the North.*

—SIR THOMAS BROWNE,
*Pseudodoxia Epidemica*

When you cross a field
do the magnets at the center
of the Earth stop you cold,
straighten your spine, snap your head
back with centrifugal violence?
Does the iron in your blood rush to your heart?

On the street, where metal flies,
you see someone you once loved
and feel yourself drawn fiercely
in the opposite direction.
Is that because you were so much alike—
enough to repel one another after many years?

Across the steel bridge to the frozen fields,
her stiletto heels throwing sparks,
a woman slips through the dark crowd.
Her strange, hot jewelry clatters.
Smoke envelops her hair.
And suddenly, despite yourself, you're following her,
the needle in your compass spinning wildly.

# In the Year of the Comet

On the morning the comet
is to streak through
the Earth's atmosphere
for the first time
in thirty-eight years,
snow sifts from the low
clouds and the pigeons
huddle on icy ledges.
The people of the city
go about their business,
eating and drinking
and making money,
confessing to crimes
and confessing their love.
The comet last appeared
in the month I was born,
and in the intervening
years—while my life
has followed its own
erratic course—it has
traveled past Venus
and Mercury, around (and
dangerously close to)
the sun, and then out
beyond Pluto, its orbit
brushing the outer rim
of the solar system.
Now, because of the storm
blanketing this part
of North America,
I won't see it pass;
but standing by a window
with eyes closed, I still
hope to feel a tingle
in my nerve endings,
a hum of recognition
in my bloodstream,

a response of some sort
to the questions
circling in my head:
When the comet next
returns, (if I am not
dead) where will I be
as I approach eighty,
and what will I be
called on to remember
of my own life for
the benefit of others
and how much will I
have forgotten in order
to live with myself?
Will I even recall
this comet I never saw,
which hisses across
the sky at ten-forty-one
for less than a minute
before hurtling back
into space, toward the sun—
even more dangerously
close to the sun.

# About the Author

Nicholas Christopher was born in 1951, and was graduated from Harvard College. He is the author of three previous books of poems, *On Tour with Rita* (1982), *A Short History of the Island of Butterflies* (1986) and *Desperate Characters: A Novella in Verse & Other Poems* (1988). He has published a novel, *The Soloist* (1986), and he edited the anthology *Under 35: The New Generation of American Poets* (1989). He is the recipient of numerous awards, most recently the 1991 I. B. Lavan Award from the Academy of American Poets. He is a frequent contributor to *The New Yorker,* and his work has been widely published in leading magazines and literary journals and in various anthologies in the United States and abroad. He lives in New York City.